Bob the Dog

Written by
Rodrigo Folgueira

Illustrated by
Poly Bernatene

PaRragon

Bath · New York · Singapore · Hong Kong · Cologne · Delhi
Melbourne · Amsterdam · Johannesburg · Auckland · Shenzhen

Mark and Bob the Dog
were playing in the park
one day.

They were running,
and laughing so hard
that they didn't see the...

GULP!

...tiny little yellow bird.

Bob began to sob.
"Oh, I've eaten him," he cried.
"I've eaten the tiny, innocent,
little **birdy-wirdy**."

Mark tried to comfort him...

...but Bob didn't eat birds.
He sobbed and **wailed** and **howled.**

Then Bob's tummy made a strange noise.

"Tweeeeeet!"

"He's alive, Bob!" cried Mark.

And then a little voice spoke.
"My name is Jeremy.
Jeremy the Canary.
And...

...I'm hiding in here!"

And he wouldn't say
another word.

"Oh dear," said Mark.
"I think we'd better
get some help!"

Bob and Mark gathered
all their friends.

Roger the Rabbit,

Cathy the Cat,

and, of course,
Oscar the Owl.

First, Cathy the Cat tried blowing pepper up Bob's nose, to make Jeremy come out with a sneeze...

ah...ah... achOO!

But that didn't work,
it just made Bob fall over!

Next Roger the
Rabbit tried
bouncing on Bob's
belly to make
Jeremy pop out
with a burp...

bOing...

bOing...

bOing!

But that didn't work,
it just made Bob feel sick!

Then Oscar the Owl
tried shaking Bob, to make
Jeremy fall out...

whOoah...

arghhh...

blerghh!

But that didn't work either,
it just made Bob feel dizzy!

"Please!"
yelled Mark.
"Somebody help
my dog!"

Suddenly they heard a **deafening** roar.

"J-e-r-e-m-y?!"

bellowed the big canary.

"Mommy?" said Jeremy.

"You'd better believe it's Mommy!" she boomed.

Bob felt a flutter in his tummy...

...and Jeremy the Canary appeared!

"I'm sorry," he said in a small voice. "I just didn't want to clean my room."

"Well," said Mommy, "if you don't want to clean your room, you can always clean...

...Bob's room!"

And Jeremy never complained
about cleaning his own room,
ever again!